SUPER RABBIT BOY'S
TIME JUMP!

READ MORE
PRESS START!
BOOKS!

MORE BOOKS COMING SOON!

PRESS START!
SUPER RABBIT BOY'S TIME JUMP!

THOMAS
FLINTHAM

BRANCHES

SCHOLASTIC INC.

FOR STEVE, CLAIRE, AND KALEN

Copyright © 2020 by Thomas Flintham

All rights reserved. Published by Scholastic Inc., *Publishers since 1920*. SCHOLASTIC, BRANCHES, and associated logos are trademarks and/or registered trademarks of Scholastic Inc.

The publisher does not have any control over and does not assume any responsibility for author or third-party websites or their content.

Library of Congress Cataloging-in-Publication Data

Names: Flintham, Thomas, author, illustrator. | Flintham, Thomas. Press Start! ; 9.
Title: Super Rabbit Boy's time jump! / Thomas Flintham.
Description: First edition. | New York : Branches/Scholastic Inc., 2020. | Series: Press start! ; 9
Summary: Super Rabbit Boy gained his superpowers when, as a baby, he ate the magic carrot he found in the Wise Woods; now King Viking has built a time machine in order to team up with his younger self, Prince Viking, and prevent Baby Rabbit Boy from finding that carrot—so Super Rabbit Boy has to go back in time, and with help from an unexpected player, save his younger self and protect the timeline.
Identifiers: LCCN 2019041178 | ISBN 9781338568967 (paperback) | ISBN 9781338568974 (library binding) | ISBN 9781338568981 (ebk)
Subjects: LCSH: Superheroes—Juvenile fiction. | Supervillains—Juvenile fiction. | Animals—Juvenile fiction. | Time travel—Juvenile fiction. | Video games—Juvenile fiction. | CYAC: Superheroes—Fiction. | Supervillains—Fiction. | Animals—Fiction. | Time travel—Fiction. | Video games—Fiction. | LCGFT: Superhero fiction.
Classification: LCC PZ7.1.F585 Svm 2020 | DDC [Fic]—dc23
LC record available at https://lccn.loc.gov/2019041178

10 9 8 7 6   22 23 24

Printed in China   62
First edition, September 2020
Edited by Katie Carella and Alli Brydon
Book design by Christian Zelaya

TABLE OF CONTENTS

1 PRESS START!

There is a party at Carrot Castle. Everyone is celebrating Super Rabbit Boy's Super Day. A stranger has joined the fun.

HAPPY SUPER DAY!

What is Super Day?

It's the anniversary of the day Super Rabbit Boy got his superpowers!

3

ONE NIGHT, BABY RABBIT BOY WAS HUNGRY.
SO HE CRAWLED INTO THE WISE WOODS TO
FIND SOMETHING TO EAT.

BUT THEN HE FELL INTO A HOLE IN THE
GROUND, INTO A SPECIAL BONUS MAZE LEVEL!

HE CRAWLED AROUND A TANGLE
OF UNDERGROUND TUNNELS.

HE CRAWLED THROUGH A MISTY FOREST.

THEN HE CRAWLED ACROSS A VERY HIGH
BRIDGE.

FINALLY, IN THE VERY CENTER OF THE MAZE, BABY RABBIT BOY FOUND A CARROT TO EAT.

BUT IT WAS NO ORDINARY CARROT. IT WAS A SUPER CARROT! BABY RABBIT BOY ATE THE SUPER CARROT AND IT GAVE HIM SUPERPOWERS!

The stranger takes off his disguise. It is that meanie, King Viking!

Thank you for telling me your story, Stinky Rabbit Boy. That is everything I needed to know!

What trouble are you up to now?

I've had enough of you stopping all my brilliant evil plans. So, I have come up with a SUPER brilliant evil plan!

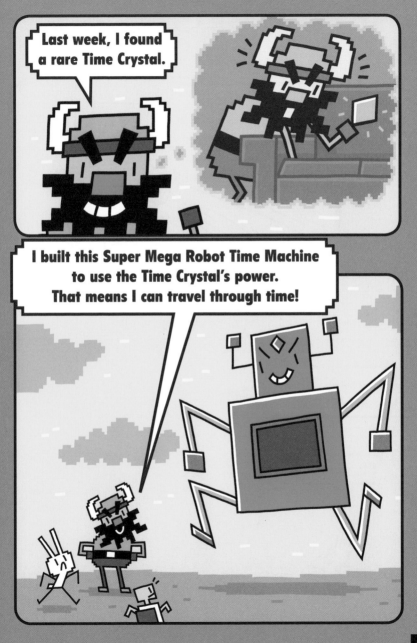

King Viking jumps into his Super Mega
Robot Time Machine.

King Viking and his time machine
disappear in a flash of light.

Has time run out for Super Rabbit Boy?

2 TIME FOR ADVENTURE

King Viking has ruined Super Rabbit Boy's Super Day party.

Super Rabbit Boy tests his Super Jump.

I still have my superpowers!

That means it isn't too late to stop King Viking from taking them away.

Super Rabbit Boy leaves for Gloom Gloom Swamp, home of Tolver the Wizard.

13

Super Rabbit Boy finally arrives. He can see Tolver's Treehouse.

I hope Tolver can help me go back in time and stop King Viking . . . before it's too late!

Super Rabbit Boy hops up to Tolver's door.

Hello! Is anyone home?

Come in, Super Rabbit Boy. I have been waiting for you!

Super Rabbit Boy tells him all about King Viking's plan.

It is another Time Crystal.

We can send you back in time, too!

Hooray!

Do we need to build a time machine, like King Viking did?

No! My magic will help us use the Time Crystal's power.

17

Tolver hands Super Rabbit Boy the Time Crystal.

Tolver casts the spell, and Super Rabbit Boy disappears in a flash of light!

3 ZOOM TO THE PAST

Super Rabbit Boy zooms back in time!

Boing! Boing! Here I go!

When the spinning stops, Super Rabbit Boy opens his eyes.

Wow! It worked! I'm in the Wise Woods — in the past!

Super Rabbit Boy looks for Baby Rabbit Boy. He spots him crawling through the woods.

There I am! Aww, I was cute!

Boo boo ba!

Now he just needs to keep Baby Rabbit Boy safe from King Viking.

Super Rabbit Boy doesn't have a chance to catch up. Baby Rabbit Boy falls down a hole!

Super Rabbit Boy jumps in.

Super Rabbit Boy lands in an underground tunnel. Baby Rabbit Boy is nowhere to be seen.

He starts searching the tunnels. They twist and turn, this way and that way.

Finally, he can hear Baby Rabbit Boy.

Super Rabbit Boy runs around a corner and quickly comes to a stop.

Super Rabbit Boy jumps into action. He must keep Baby Rabbit Boy safe! He bounces on top of King Viking's robots. They fall apart.

Super Rabbit Boy has beaten all of the robots.

He has disappeared again!

Super Rabbit Boy searches for Baby Rabbit Boy. He finds a doorway into a Misty Forest.

Super Rabbit Boy spots Baby Rabbit Boy crawling straight into a set of King Viking's traps!

5 TRAP TROUBLE!

A giant cage is about to fall on top of Baby Rabbit Boy! Super Rabbit Boy rushes forward.

Super Rabbit Boy bashes the cage away, just in time!

Baby Rabbit Boy keeps crawling. Now he's heading toward a shower of fireballs!

Super Rabbit Boy jumps into a nearby puddle. The water splashes the fireballs and they fizzle out.

Super Rabbit Boy grabs Baby Rabbit Boy.

Super Rabbit Boy and Baby Rabbit Boy bounce past more of King Viking's traps.

Finally, they reach the end of the Misty Forest. Super Rabbit Boy has kept Baby Rabbit Boy safe!

They step onto the very high bridge.

6 TIME TRICKS

A giant robot lands on the bridge in front of them. It's the Super Mega Robot Time Machine. King Viking is inside!

How did you follow me into the past?

I'd go anywhere to stop you! I won't let you take away my superpowers!

Super Rabbit Boy needs to stop King Viking and his Super Mega Robot. It's time to use his Super Jump while he still can. He jumps into the air, ready for a battle.

But he is caught by another giant robot!
A young Viking is inside.

This is Prince Viking, the younger version of me. I thought he'd have fun helping me carry out my SUPER brilliant evil plan!

43

Suddenly Super Rabbit Boy has an idea!

I just need to think about the future! If I can't beat you on my own . . .

. . . maybe I can help!

It's Super Rabbit Man — an all-grown-up Super Rabbit Boy from the future!

7 BACK FROM THE FUTURE

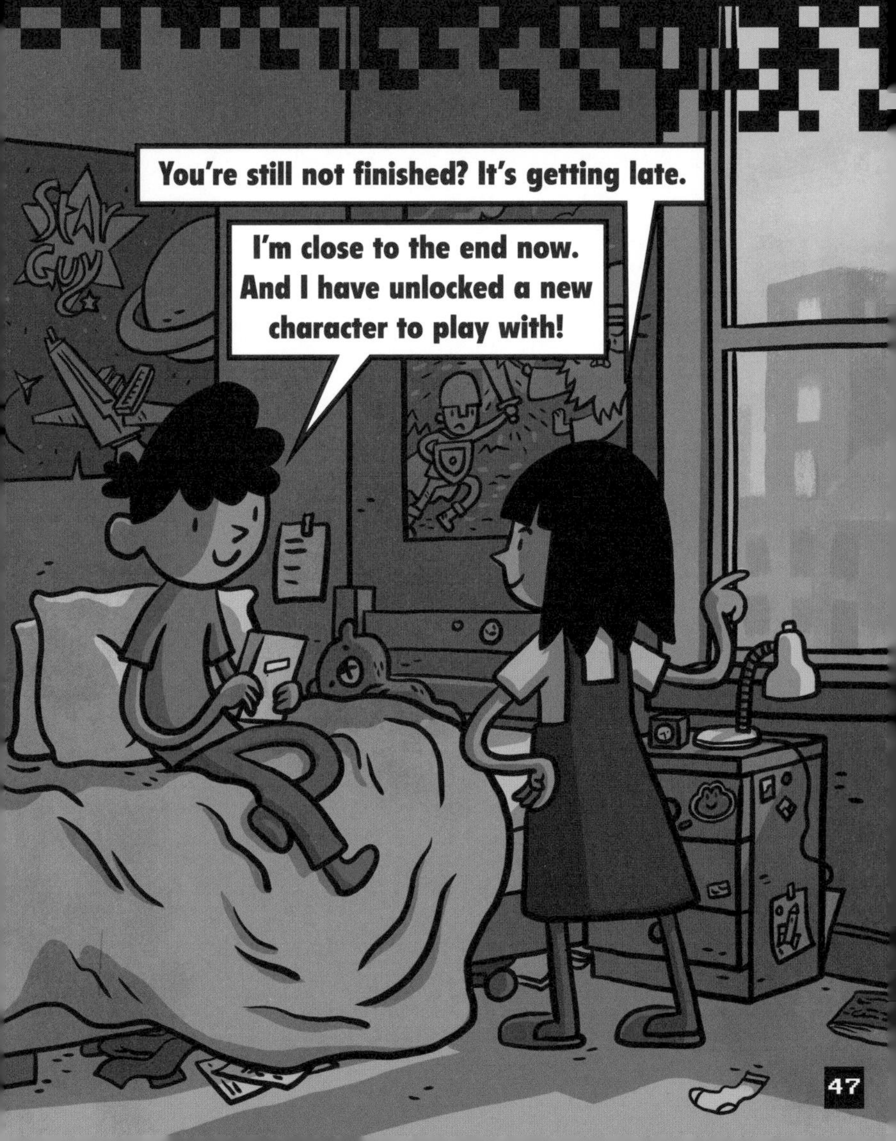

Super Rabbit Man jumps into action. He can jump really, really high — even higher than Super Rabbit Boy!

Super Rabbit Man zooms toward the two Vikings.

Super Rabbit Man bounces between the two robots.

He pushes the robot time machines to the edge of the bridge, and . . .

. . . he pushes them off! The robot time machines fall, but King Viking and Prince Viking jump out of them to safety.

Wah!

Wah! We needed those Mega Robots to stop you stinky rabbits!

Super Rabbit Man has saved the day!

51

It's Old King Viking inside <u>another</u> time machine robot!

I had to wait a long time for my Time Crystal to recharge. But it gave me time to build this Ultra Robot Boss! It is unbeatable.

Wow! That's a cool robot!

I'm even smarter than I thought!

Super Rabbit Boy and Super Rabbit Man are worried. They could still lose their superpowers!

The two heroes hop into action.

The Ultra Robot Boss easily grabs
Super Rabbit Boy and Super Rabbit Man.

Super Rabbit Boy sees the first hint of sunrise. They don't have much time! They still haven't gotten Baby Rabbit Boy to the Super Carrot.

A mysterious blur speeds through the air. It bounces all around Old King Viking's Ultra Robot Boss.

Wah! What's happening?!

9 THE OLD TIMER

The Ultra Robot Boss falls to pieces. Super Rabbit Boy and Super Rabbit Man are free!

My Ultra Robot Boss should have been unbeatable! Who did that?

It's Super Rabbit Gramps!

But Old King Viking is up to something.
He searches through broken robot parts.

Super Rabbit Gramps holds up Old King Viking's Time Crystal.

Super Rabbit Gramps throws the Time Crystal against the floor. It shatters.

King Viking and Old King Viking, you will never travel back in time again.

When the Time Crystal smashes, King Viking and Old King Viking disappear in a flash of light!

Wah! Where did they go?

King Viking and Old King Viking are sent zooming back to their own times.

As soon as my Time Crystal has recharged, I'm going to go back in time again and win!

You young fool! That is what I thought when I was your age! But look at me now!

Prince Viking runs away from the three heroes.

You stinky rabbits! I'm going to become the best bad guy ever. One day I'll get you for this!

64

The rabbits have stopped King Viking's plan!

Super Rabbit Boy suddenly realizes someone is missing . . .

The heroes need to get Baby Rabbit Boy to the Super Carrot. They're almost out of time!

They start looking everywhere!

Super Rabbit Gramps finds something.

Baby Rabbit Boy has found the Super Carrot! He eats it and gets his superpowers.

CHOMP!

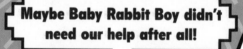

Maybe Baby Rabbit Boy didn't need our help after all!

As the sun rises, Baby Rabbit Boy settles
down for a nap. And the three heroes zoom
back to their own times.

Your ten minutes is up. Time to go to sleep, Sunny. Sunny?
Good night, kiddo.
THE END

THOMAS FLINTHAM

has always loved to draw and tell stories, and now that is his job! He grew up in Lincoln, England, and studied illustration in Camberwell, London. He lives by the sea with his wife, Bethany, in Cornwall.

Thomas is the creator of THOMAS FLINTHAM'S BOOK OF MAZES AND PUZZLES and many other books for kids. PRESS START! is his first early chapter book series.

Super Rabbit Boy is zooming back through time. He is ready to stop King Viking's next evil plan. Can you help him find his way back to the King Viking from the present day?

PRESS START!

How much do you know about

SUPER RABBIT BOY'S TIME JUMP?

Everyone is having a party for Super Rabbit Boy's Super Day. What exactly are they celebrating?

Who is the stranger who asks to hear about how Super Rabbit Boy got his superpowers? Why does he ask?

Super Rabbit Boy has to follow King Viking back in time. Who does he go see for help with this? And what does Super Rabbit Boy need in order to time travel?

In Chapter 9, who comes in to save Super Rabbit Boy and Super Rabbit Man?

Super Rabbit Boy has Baby Rabbit Boy, Super Rabbit Man, and Super Rabbit Gramps to help him on his quest. What would your superhero team look like? Write and draw your own action story.